This book is dedicated to my Sun Cody. Being your mother is everything! My heart treasures every moment spent learning, loving and growing with you.

Celebrate Your Magic is an offering to the Divine. May I continue to be an instrument for your loving creations. I AM your heart and hands in this world! I am all in!

"Celebrate Your Magic" - First edition
Published in 2021 by Jacqueline Rolandelli

ISBN paperback 978-1-7374477-1-9
ISBN hardback 978-1-7374477-0-2

CELEBRATE YOUR MAGIC

Jacqueline Hyacinth

art by
Stella Maris Mongodi

Our car is packed and we are ready to hit the road. Mom and I are headed up to the mountains where we will camp for a few days.

We love taking long drives together. Mom makes up silly songs and we laugh till our faces hurt.

My name is Nasir. I live with my mom, and our three cats, Lilly, Jade, and Buddha. My dad lives at his own house. My most favorite thing to do is draw and paint.

Ever since I was very little, I felt that I was different from others. I can sense what people are thinking and feeling. Mom says I have the gift of knowing, just like my grandmother.

I don't have many friends at school, so I spend a lot of time alone.

Last week during recess, Jimmy Valance and his crew surrounded me on the playground and threatened me. I was so embarrassed, everyone was watching. When they call me names, it really hurts.

I am tired of hiding who I am. What can I say, I dance to my own beat!

Today I am going to be brave and share a secret with you. Here goes, are you ready?

Promise not to laugh!

I have magic powers and I can communicate with animals. I know, I know! Can you believe it?

But it is true and maybe you have this gift too.

Come along on an adventure with me! Let's go!

We headed down Eden Trail and made it to our campsite. We set up tent under a huge oak tree.

High fives, mom!

Mom lied on her fancy chair to read her book.

"Mom, can I go down to the lake?" "Yes, Nasir, just wear your shoes."

I threw on my favorite magic cheetah slippers that my dad gave me. When I wear them, I instantly have more courage and I feel like I can do anything. I become a Mystical Magician! Any fear disappears and my spirit comes alive with adventure. Do you have something that you wear that makes you feel like you can do anything?

As I approached the lake, I saw a family of white swans gliding across the water. They were so majestic.

I opened my heart, closed my eyes, and took a deep breath and from inside my body, I called the swans to come to me.

Within seconds, one of the swans was at the water's edge. He motioned to me with his neck to get on. He was warm and his feathers were soft. As we drifted across the water, I felt our hearts become one. All of my worries disappeared.

After a magnificent ride, the swan took me back to land. I thanked him for his kindness.

He said, "My name is Cygnus. Whenever you need me, all you have to do is call upon me with your heart. I am your spirit guide, here to bring wisdom and peace throughout your life." Then he drifted away into the light of the shimmering water.

While walking back to the campsite I heard howling coming from the woods. Within moments a family of wolves surrounded me.

I was frightened but I knew I couldn't outrun them and I had to stand my ground. I took a deep breath, looked down at my magic slippers, and began to growl and stomp my feet.

The alpha wolf stepped forward and encircled me, sniffing me out. Our eyes met and a fire ignited in my body. The wolves howled, ah-whooo and I howled back. Ah-whooo. There was a power growing deep within me, a confidence I never felt before.

The Shewolf licked my face and said, "You have demonstrated bravery, you are one of us now. My name is Leto, guardian of children. If you ever feel afraid, all you have to do is call upon me with your heart. I am your spirit guide, here to bring fierce courage and empowerment to guide you throughout your life." Then the wolves disappeared into the light of the sun.

I heard the branches shaking in the tree above me. A monkey swung down from one of the limbs and touched my face. Then an even bigger one hooted and jumped toward us.

The elder monkey pulled me up and I sat beside him. He was gentle and he made funny noises when I rubbed his belly.

"You are Nasir!" He poked my chest and my heart beat like a drum. "The panther told me of the prophecy. A young magician will come forth with the gift of communicating with the animals."

Holy moly! Who is this panther and what is going on with these magic slippers? I wondered.

The monkey placed his paw on my head and said, "My name is Hanuman. Whenever you feel alone, all you have to do is call upon me with your heart. I am your spirit guide, here to bring joy and victory throughout your life." Then the monkeys disappeared into the light of the sun.

Mom yelled up from below, "Nasir, can I come up and visit with you?" "Of course!", I said.

Mom climbed the tree. After my visits with the swans, wolves, and monkeys, my heart was full of love.

Humans don't understand me like animals do. I notice that animals have big families that stay together. Human families sometimes separate, like my mom and dad did.

Mom leaned in and gave me a warm hug. "Nasir", she said, "you have a heart that can hold the whole world."

We climbed down the tree and walked through the forest. I saw a shadow on my left and sensed we weren't alone. I used my power to intuit if we were in danger.

Out of the corner of my eye I could see a black panther tracking us.

I remembered my conversation with Hanuman. I steadied my breath, slowed my steps, closed my eyes and opened my heart and asked, "Why are you following me?"

She replied, "I have come to bring support and courage to your mother."

I turned toward the panther. Mom turned too. She kneeled down on the earth and bowed her head. The panther moved closer and placed her head on Mom's shoulder and they embraced.

Mom's eyes filled with tears, and with pride she said, "Nasir, this is my spirit guide Bastet. She has been guiding me since I was a little girl. She protected me all my life and has brought me strength and friendship."

I was shocked to discover that mom is like me, and we both have magic powers. Bastet invited me to get on her back and we all walked back to our campsite.

As I snuggled up by the campfire, I replayed all the adventures of the day in my mind.

I must be the luckiest boy in the world. I have a mom and dad who love me and a family of animal spirits to guide me throughout my life.

I believe that the key to my magic is trusting my heart and embracing my unique gifts.

I thought about the times I had wished I was like everyone else and how I felt afraid to reveal my true self.

Not anymore! I Am Nasir, and I am wonderful just the way I am. From now on I will **Celebrate My Magic**!

To my Mother and Father, Geraldine and Stephen, thank you
for this precious life. Your love was the soil for my soul.

Cody, you are my muse! Your soul inspires me to love deeper, shine
brighter and show up in every way.

Bachier, you are my chosen sun from another Mother. I love you!

Stella, my magic illustrator! Thank you for being my partner and seeing
my hearts vision!

Michelle, my word weaving wizard, you are a brilliant editor.

Christine, it was a joy strengthening our sisterhood through this book.

Mirjam, my soul sister. Thank you for always seeing and believing in me.

Carine, my teacher. Light of my Light! Thank you for walking me home.

To all of my incredible friends, thank you for your love and support.

Divine Mother, thank you for my life. To my ancestors and my Sai family,
I stand on your shoulders. To all of the animal spirits, angels and guides
who walk with our family, I bow. We love and appreciate you!

Jacqueline Hyacinth

is a mother, author, mystic, and spiritual teacher from New York. For ten years she has served families through spiritual counseling, rites of passage, and healing work. Jacqueline is now weaving simple teachings through storytelling, spreading messages of love, trust, truth, courage, health, and acceptance.

She draws on ancient knowledge to uplift the modern family and keep the magic legacy alive. Jacqueline has a vision that our little people are supported to be leaders and earth guardians.

When Jacqueline isn't writing you can find her traveling, drumming and singing, and communing with nature.

Check Nasir's awesome merchandise at:
www. celebrateyourmagic.com
and connect on Instagram @celebrateyourmagic

Stella Maris Mongodi

was born in Italy but now lives in Edinburgh. She got her degree in Ancient theatre, while studying art and illustration for many years with renowned professionals such as Alessandra Cimatoribus, Anna Castagnoli, Carll Cneut and Stefano Moroni.

Even though she started with oil colors, acrylics and watercolors, her illustrations are now entirely digital, but they still have a "traditional media flavor" characterized by a dreamy, feathery and still playful style. She loves owls and mice, sewing colorful crazy skirts and skating (although she's very bad at it).

You can find more at www.stellamarisart.it or you can connect on Instagram @stellamaris_illustrator.

CPSIA information can be obtained
at www.ICGtesting.com
Printed in the USA
LVHW070948270821
696262LV00003B/86